# Mind Melt and Other Stories

# Femdom Mind Control

# Flash Fiction – Vol. 37

## S.B.

Copyright © 2022 by S.B.

All Rights Reserved.

Cover Design by S.B.

(Photo by Jason Leung on Unsplash)

## Disclaimer

This is a work of fiction. Names, characters, business, events, and incidents are the products of the author's imagination. Any resemblance to actual persons, living or dead, or actual events is purely coincidental. All characters are over 18.

# Table of Contents


◎ Catching Up - 7
◎ Her Playground - 10
◎ His One Weakness - 13
◎ Impossible Castle - 16
◎ Meg's Diet - 20
◎ Mind Melt - 23
◎ Not Like This - 28
◎ Perfect Ass - 31
◎ Speedrun Into Submission - 34
◎ Surprise Party - 39
◎ The Hypnotist Always Wins - 43
◎ You Are Not Mind-Controlled - 48

*Surrender now.*

*Thank you to all patrons of Spell... B-O-U-N-D.*

# Catching Up

Anne checked her watch for the thousandth time, mentally counting the seconds until Patricia's arrival. It had been almost four years since the last time they were together, and she could barely contain the excitement. No one understood the ways of her mind like Patricia. She was the reason she had become such a horny hypno-slut.

The two had met in Memphis, following troubled times for both. Anne was coming out of a divorce after realizing no man could ever make her happy, and Patricia had recently been fired from the job she loved the most. After sitting next to one another at a bar for almost half an hour drinking their favorite poison all alone, they discovered the joy of sharing their misery together, and one thing led to another until they were pushing the limits of the hotel bed. It was the beginning of a beautiful relationship.

Hypnosis became a part of it about three months after the first drink and all because Anne found a pair of glowing contact lenses inside her girlfriend's purse.

"What do you use these for?" she asked.

"To melt the minds of whoever I want," Patricia purred.

"I'm serious."

"So am I. Nothing compares to the thrill of putting someone under and then guiding their mind through the kinky scenario of my choice."

"Really? Why didn't you tell me about this sooner?"

"I was waiting for the right moment, but it seems you took care of that for me. What do you say, Anne? Shall we get wild tonight?"

"You want to hypnotize me?"

"I would love to, but I won't push you if you're not up for it. Still, I think you'd be a wonderful subject."

"Why?"

"It's the way you feel things, hun. You have quite the imagination, and that's almost mandatory for a riveting experience. Come on, let me guide you to pleasures you never thought possible. Just say yes."

Yes. One time. Two times. Ten times and more. After a while, the numbers became meaningless, her mind drifting in a current of triggers and post-hypnotic suggestions. She remembered a few but was oblivious to the rest. Patricia played with her memories like a harp, always knowing which string to pluck to get the results she wanted. Perfection was always on finger snap away and it seemed nothing could stand in the way of their mesmerizing adventure.

Nothing except time.

Two years went by, and Patricia slowly found herself looking for something else, a search that culminated in a job offer overseas. They tried to make it work at first, but the different time zones and overall distance between them eventually took their toll. The separation was amicable, but not everything faded. Anne thought of her every single day, sometimes dreaming herself into a trance hoping to relive those wonderful moments of surrender again. Thankfully, the wait was almost over.

Patricia arrived at her doorstep five minutes past the scheduled time. The tall brunette of Asian descent looked as enticing as ever, sporting a slim-fit velvet dress similar to the one she wore on their first encounter. Even the style of make-up was the same, which triggered an obvious emotional response.

"Honey, I'm back," the hypnotist said, staring at her former lover with her gorgeous brown eyes. In her right hand, she held a box with a pair of shiny lenses.

"It's wonderful to see you," Anne hugged her. "But if you think we're going to pick up immediately where we left off just like that, you're..."

"Absolutely right?" Patricia ground her breasts against hers, lips dangerously close to a wet kiss. "How many of your old triggers still work?"

"N-none," Anne gasped as a violet-painted fingernail caressed her right ear lobe.

"You were always a terrible liar. I left my bags in the elevator. Go get them for me, slut."

"You can't just command me like..."

"Now!" Patricia snapped her fingers and smiled as the trance addict's mind unraveled before her. They had a lot of catching up to do.

# Her Playground

Lucas opened his eyes and stared in every direction, seeing nothing but pure blackness. A throbbing pain hammered the back of his head. Touching it, he felt the warm blood slide down his fingers. What the hell had happened?

As he contemplated the dark surroundings, flashes of broken memories came back to haunt him. The night out with his friend Harry and girlfriend Joan... the mysterious redhead woman they had tried to hook him up with... her infectious laughter as she blew a puff of pink smoke into his eyes and nostrils... the back of her car and then nothing. The story told by those glimpses was clear, and yet he was having a hard time believing it to be true.

"Come on, there's no way you were kidnapped," he said to himself.

"I wouldn't be so sure about that," a sultry, feminine voice echoed from parts unknown as if she had read his mind. It was the same voice as the redhead woman. The way she pronounced her Rs was unmistakable. What was her name again? Angel? Angela? No, Angelina! That was it.

"Where...? Where am I?"

"Welcome to my playground, Lucas," Angelina replied. "I hope you have what it takes to entertain me."

"Angelina? Is that you? What's going on? Where are my friends?"

"Back in their place, I think. They were quite happy when you decided to stay talking to me a while longer. Of course, they didn't know what truly was going on and they don't have to. The rest of this night is just for us."

"You... you drugged me..." he slurred. "Why?"

"You probably wouldn't have agreed to follow me here otherwise. I'm a woman of... special tastes, Lucas, and when I see something or someone I like, I take it. Are you ready to see what I have in store for you?"

The moment she finished talking, a luminous explosion bathed the space he was in revealing a metallic alcove with a half-open that led into a sprawling labyrinth adorned with spiraling walls. It was at least the size of a football field, with a black ceiling blocking all external sources of light. A giant warehouse, perhaps? He didn't know, and his gut was telling him it was best not to find out.

"What do you want, Angelina?"

"I want to have a little fun with you. Do you know what amuses me the most, Lucas? To make men so desperate they'll do anything to please me. The trapped ones are the best, scurrying around my little maze, like rats. It's your turn. You stand at the threshold of a treat like no other, purposely created to drain every ounce of resistance from my subjects while I watch. There's a way out, of course, but no one has ever resisted long enough to find it. How far can you go without losing your mind?"

"As far I must. I will get out of here!"

"Will you really? I'll love to watch you try. Go on, my little mouse. Show me how strong you are."

Lucas got up and peered beyond the door's threshold. The labyrinth was like a horrible acid trip, filled with intersecting corridors and dead ends. The ever-moving patterns on the cold walls defied his sense of reality and he could swear there were living, breathing shadows waiting for him in every corner. Whatever she had drugged him was still very much present in his system, giving every aspect of his surrounding an ethereal, dream-like quality that hurt his brain.

He stepped forward, hugging the right side. No one would believe this shit was real, but when he got out... Oh, when he got out...

"You're going to pay for this, bitch!"

"Let's see if you still stay that when you're on your knees, begging for a sliver of attention."

Lucas grimaced and dove deeper into the bowels of her madness, hoping to come out victorious in the end.

He never did.

# His One Weakness

Damian Rivers was a successful man in every sense of the word. He was only fourteen when he invented a revolutionary chip that advanced the computer industry thirty years minimum. At sixteen, he was already a multi-millionaire, and less than a year later, his company featured prominently in the Fortune 500. Before he was old enough to drink, he had already sold the company for three times more than it was worth, and on the day of his 22nd birthday, he started a new venture that was even more successful than the first. The thirst for his inventive mind was real, and there was no way of telling when or if his winning streak would ever end.

In the eyes of both the public and his most direct competitors, it seemed Damian could do no wrong, but every man has a weakness no matter how much they try to hide it. His was known only by a select group of people, yet it only takes one bad apple to spoil the whole barrel. Damian was addicted to hypnotic eyes and his assistant Timothy had someone he was dying to introduce him to.

Her name was Erica, a buxom redhead with a freckled nose and an impish smile. She was obviously pushing thirty and wore a complete black leather ensemble like a biker chick from Hell. On his mental scale, 'average-looking' was the right word to describe her, no more than a six in ten, but what she lacked in overall beauty was compensated by her crystalline blue eyes.

"Charmed, I'm sure," she said as she waltzed inside his office, with Timothy smiling sheepishly by the door. "You did well, Tim. You may leave us now."

"Yes, Erica," he muttered and locked the door behind him, to the utmost surprise of the tech wizard.

"So, you're the friend he can't stop talking about, huh?" Damian noted, unconsciously drawn to her penetrating stare.

"Friend is not exactly the word I'd use to describe our relationship, but yes, that's me," she purred. "Before you ask, no, I don't follow your work, nor I'm one of those obsessed fans who would do anything to be where I am right now. Still, I wanted to meet you and I'm glad we finally have the chance to do so."

"Why are you here?"

"Because you need me, of course. You like something I have, and you have something I like. Don't you ever get tired of being so rich, Damian? Wouldn't it be better to put that money to good use?"

"You mean like a charity? Because you don't look like one, my dear."

Erica slid to his desk and took a seat on it, legs spread seductively across its length. Her long red hair fell forward but didn't obscure the impossibly attractive gaze that had already completely engulfed his senses.

"You're right, I'm not, but you're mine. Timothy told me all about your Internet searches and the videos you store on your hard drive. You dream of gorgeous eyes ransacking your mind. I've come to tell you it's time to stop dreaming."

Damian pursed his lips as her ravenous eyes fell on him, unrelenting in their devouring intent. They would not stop while he still had thoughts left but, like with so many other pets that had come before, his resistance was to be brief. Peeping at the door, Timothy jerked his cock in sync with his boss's dwindling mind before they both exploded in a sea of white. The man with too much money in his life was about to get a lot poorer.

## Impossible Castle

Oliver wiped the sweat off his furrowed brow and glanced at the camera drone assigned to follow him during the last portion of his wondrous quest. Throughout the years, Impossible Castle had seen many contestants come and go. Usually, the audience's favorites were the first to be eliminated, with the most disliked characters surviving long enough to get a chance at redemption. However, the fantasy contest's name hadn't come by accident. In over twenty editions, no one had ever made it to the end.

The ever-changing challenge comprised hundreds of rooms filled with traps, devious puzzles, and even brutal combat against heavily armored foes. It was not a competition for the faint of heart and anyone that tried to say otherwise was bound to get an axe to the head five minutes after setting foot on the main hub. Oliver, a.k.a. Crimson Warrior of the Flame of Darn had defied the producer's expectations from day one with his cunning observation skills and propensity to think outside of the box. His rapid reflexes had also saved him from imminent death on at least three separate occasions, all of which had been incredibly nerve-racking.

Now, after dozens of hours of punishing entertainment, Oliver had reached the final gauntlet known as the Spiral Hall. Beyond it, laid the domains of Queen Elianthe, Mistress of the Impossible Castle. It was said that her eyes were like giant diamonds capable of hypnotizing anyone that stared at them for too long, but he was ready for her. No one would keep the one-million-dollar prize money away from him.

Oliver ventured into the hall, weapons at the ready for whatever came his way. The room was set atop an undulating platform designed to disconcert the unwary contestants. The spiraling patterns on the wall shifted with each step allowing for otherwise unseen foes to emerge from the shadows for a strike. He glimpsed the first one's blade before he made a move, but the two that followed almost ended his run. Blocking the attacks with his curved blade, he kicked the first back into the abyss before pushing the hilt of the sword into the throat of the second. Two more foes came at him from behind yet were easily put to the ground. In the control room right above the main set, the show's producers wondered if the Impossible Castle was about to become possible after all.

The golden doors at the end of the hall creaked as Oliver opened them far and wide and saw the result of stellar costume design brought to life. Elianthe was every man and woman's wet dream with her long flowing dark robe that highlighted her cleavage rather than trying to hide it. The diadem on her forehead glowed with unnatural intensity, and it was almost as beautiful as her pure, reflective eyes.

"A wandering fool has finally made it to my throne room," Laetitia, the actress playing the role chewed the scenery with gusto. "Two choices now stand before you now. Eternal servitude or death. What will you choose?"

"Neither" Oliver dashed forward. "I choose to slay you and conquer the secrets of this castle once and for all. Begone, witch!"

"You choose what you can never have, as all fools do. Come and face your destiny, then."

Oliver swung his sword her way, with real-time digital effects overlaying the tip to create the illusion of exploding magical lightning. Elianthe smirked at the nearest camera and raised her arms in the air, creating a massive luminous burst that lit the entire set.

"What the hell was that?" the show's main writer asked in the control room. "Did you add new powers to Elianthe without telling me?"

"That wasn't us..." the head of the VFX team cocked his head, "... and these readings are... oh, my God!"

"What are you saying?"

"I think we just saw real magic live on camera."

"Impossible!"

"Is it?"

Below their feet, "Elianthe" was now floating mid-air, a never seen trinket hanging from her supple neck. Laetitia always knew her grandmother's old emerald pendant would be her ticket to fame, glory, and power beyond measure, and what better way to make her presence felt in the world than before a live audience the size of the whole European continent?

Oliver covered his eyes, blinded by the devastating shock wave that was to change the fate of the known world forever. The Impossible Castle would not be vanquished that night or any other, for soon there would be no one free to even try. Long live Queen Laetitia, Mistress of the Universe!

# Meg's Diet

Monday

I finally did it! I caved in. I was so fucking tired of hearing Meg rave about those diet pills of hers that I bought a box. I don't believe they'll work as she claims though I'll give her the benefit of the doubt for now. I could stand to lose a few pounds to feel good about myself again. If I shed one pound a week without additional morning exercises, that would be great, but we'll see. The pink tablets are waiting for me. Wish me luck.

Tuesday

Three in the morning, three before bedtime. It seems overkill to have so many of these a day but apparently, that's how it goes. Meg was over the moon when I told her the news and is looking forward to seeing how I progress. It's too early to pass any judgment, of course, but I can tell you this: the taste they leave in the mouth is as sweet as it gets. Perhaps that's its biggest secret. Will I still be tempted to eat sugary treats if it feels like my mouth is already full of them? Hmmm...

Wednesday

What the hell? Did I lose half a pound overnight? How? I seriously don't get how I burned calories while I was asleep, but okay. I guess this shit works, but I'm still not sure whether that's a good or a bad thing. Now, where did I leave my water bottle? It's time for my daily fix again.

Thursday

I lost another half a pound last night and I'm starting to see certain shapes in my body that I believe to be long gone. To say I'm impressed with this regimen is an understatement, but things are far from perfect. This aftertaste is fucking relentless, and I seem to have headaches all the time now. Meg says that such side effects are common and will wear off as my body gets accustomed to the pill's formula. Speaking of that, there are two key ingredients for which I can't find a single description online, which is definitely odd. I'm starting to wonder if this is FDA-approved or not, but I won't stop now. I need to see if these promising results hold up at the end of the week. I sure hope so.

Friday

Another pound down overnight and I'm at a complete loss for words. The headaches didn't go away and the sweetness in my mouth remains as insufferable as ever. Overall, I feel good, but also a little... empty. I asked Meg if these things can cause addiction and she simply grinned. I don't know how to interpret her reaction, and not sure if I should bother. I'm going to grab dinner now and then wrap up the day. Until tomorrow.


Saturday


I... I... Fuck! This hurts like hell! I had the worst night in my life. The scale tells me I lost another pound, but I feel like I lost a lot more than that. My thoughts are all jumbled, and I can hardly breathe. It's hard to describe, but it's almost like my brain was tossed inside an active volcano and is now melting away. I need to call Meg to see if she knows what's happening to me. I... I...


Sunday


I'm good. I'm perfect. I'll never be better for as long as I live. Meg came to me this morning and made my purpose clear. I'm her slave. I've always been her slave. I'll always be her slave. Her pills flattened my stomach and my mind. I see and accept the truth now. The headaches are no more, but the sweet taste of slavery is everlasting. I'll have my dose now, thank you. You should do the same.

# Mind Melt

"Good morning, Robert. This is your wake-up call, courtesy of MindMelt Industries, Inc. Thank you for subscribing to our service. You are hereby reminded that you are to listen to our Motivational Mantra Set while you shower, have breakfast, and head out to work. Don't forget your wireless headphones and have a wonderful day."

(...)

"Good afternoon, Robert. This is our second warning of the day, courtesy of MindMelt Industries, Inc. Your training plan also includes listening to our Energy Booster Package. This selection will begin in approximately ten seconds and last the entirety of your lunch break. Take a deep breath and relax so this experience can be more pleasurable, overall. We hope you continue to have a wonderful day."

(...)

"Good evening, Robert. This is your third notice, courtesy of MindMelt Industries, Inc. After a long day at work, there's nothing better than to relax to the sounds of our Nocturnal Fantasies Bundle. We will play the first volume between now and the time you go to bed, with Volumes Two, Three, and Four, accompanying you during your dreams. This is sure to make you feel like a better man, so enjoy. Have a wonderful night."

(...)

"Good morning, Robert. This is your wake-up call again, courtesy of MindMelt Industries, Inc. Just like yesterday, the Motivational Mantra Set will be your guide in the next hour. Listen to it attentively and be sure to absorb every word. Have a wonderful day."

(...)

"Good afternoon, Robert. This is your second reminder, courtesy of MindMelt Industries, Inc. The Energy Booster Package is ready for activation. Do not allow yourself to get distracted from it for maximum results. Have a wonderful day."

(...)

"Good evening, Robert. Your third warning is here, courtesy of MindMelt Industries, Inc. Our data shows you've responded very well to the Nocturnal Fantasies

Bundle yesterday, so we'll be including Volume Five in the selection today. Do not remove your headphones when you go to bed. We hope you continue on your path to improvement. Have a wonderful night."

(...)

"Good morning, Robert. These are your morning instructions, courtesy of MindMelt Industries, Inc. You will listen to the Motivational Mantra Set as usual, but also incorporate the first installment of Positive Thoughts in your playlist. This adds another ten minutes to your training, but I'm sure that's not a problem for you. Have a wonderful day."

(...)

"Good afternoon, Robert. This is your second notice, courtesy of MindMelt Industries, Inc. You must continue to listen to our Energy Booster Package, and feel free to recommend it to anyone you talk to during the day. Relax and enjoy yourself. Have a wonderful day."

(...)

"Good evening, Robert. This is your third warning, courtesy of MindMelt Industries, Inc. You talked to ten different people about our services and that's good, but we know you can do better. Tomorrow, you will aim to double that number. In the meantime, you are to experience the best night of your life, surrounded by our Nocturnal Fantasies Bundle. We know what you want, and we will give it to you. Have a wonderful night."

(...)

"Good morning, Robert. MindMelt Industries, Inc commands you to listen to the Motivational Mantra Set. Do it now. Have a wonderful day."

(...)

"Good afternoon, Robert. MindMelt Industries, Inc. commands you to listen to the Energy Booster Package right away. Obey. Have a wonderful day."

(...)

"Good evening, Robert. MindMelt Industries, Inc is pleased with your contribution to our cause. You spoke to twenty-five different people and five of them are subscribed to our services now. They will receive similar training to yours and become what they're meant to be. After tonight, your real purpose will become perfectly crystallized in your mind. Listen to the Nocturnal Fantasies Bundle and accept the path you are to walk on for the rest of your life. Have a wonderful night."

(...)

"Good morning, slave. Henceforth, your mind and body are the exclusive property of MindMelt Industries, Inc. You work for us. You will continue to spread the word about our products, and praise our CEO, the divine Harriet Love at every opportunity. She is your Goddess and there will never be another before her. We will make sure your brainwashing never falters and you will yearn to go deeper and deeper for us. We own you, bitch. Now get busy and make us more money. Have a wonderful day.

## Not Like This

William shook his head and screamed at the computer screen as if the world was ending. His fury was so intense that it echoed throughout the apartment, forcing his girlfriend Anne to stop everything she was doing to check on him.

"Not like this!" he said, head buried between his shoulders.

"Why are you so upset?" she asked, peeking inside the bedroom.

"Because of this shit!" he pointed at the screen, now dominated by a bunch of cartoon characters with strange proportions. The art style was incredibly colorful and fun and yet he was miserable about it.

Anne entered the bedroom and stood behind his chair. "What am I looking at?"

"Someone decided it was a good idea to create a fucking Chibi version of *Hypnotist from Outer Space*," he grumbled. "Look at this abomination!"

"Aww… it looks cute. Can I see the trailer from the beginning?"

"Why? It sucks!"

"Indulge me, okay?"

"Fine."

He hit the 'play' button on the video and immediately looked away. It wasn't just the characters that irked him, but also the rest of the package. The voice acting - if you could call it that! - was dreadful, familiar story beats had been mutilated beyond recognition, and the soundtrack was a Frankensteinian mishmash of J-Pop and MIDI samples of old. It couldn't get any worse.

"I don't understand how they destroyed one of my favorite movies like this. The world of 'Hypnotist from Outer Space' is supposed to be sexy, not whatever this is. It's fucking gross!"

"I think you're being too hard," she kissed the back of his neck. "So, what if it's not the same soft-porn fantasy you fell in love with when you were a teen? Let them do something different with the franchise. The original will always exist for when you need a bit of... release."

"You said that on purpose, didn't you?" he glanced at her, reminiscing about the first time they had watched the movie together with genuinely explosive results.

"Of course, I did," she gently lowered her hands between his legs and started caressing his balls. "Wouldn't it be nice if you could have that right now?"

"Hmmm, yes... Can we?"

"Perhaps... on one condition."

"What is it?"

"You'll have to suffer through this Chibi rendition from beginning to end," she grinned.

"What? No! If that's the price for cumming, I'd rather not cum at all."

"Really?" she grabbed his left testicle and squeezed it between her fingers. "Because that can be arranged..."

The panic on his face became immediately clear. "Honey, that's not what I said, okay?"

"It was what I heard. Think about it... your thoughts slowly fading as I lock your mind and cock away, never to cum again without permission. Just the thought of you sacrificing your pleasure for me makes me wet," she cooed. "What do you say, big boy? Shall I make you small and obedient to my will?"

"Hmmm, well... That's tempting, but..."

"I'll wear my cosplay of the alien hypnotist if you say 'yes'."

"Fuck yes!" he leaned for a kiss as she squeezed his testicle even harder.

"I'll get ready then," she smiled as she left him hanging and sauntered away. So many months trying to convince him to embrace hypnotic chastity for her and all it took was a bastardized version of his favorite erotic movie to push him over the edge. "You're going to regret not watching the movie," she chuckled.

She was absolutely right.

# Perfect Ass

"Fuck!" Jason muttered in bed as he struggled to stop the onslaught of sexy images from flooding his brain. They were all of Marcia and from the favorite part of her anatomy. While his closest friends only cared about boobs - the bigger, the better! - his preferences had always been the same since the days of the first erection. He was an ass man through and through and hers was just...

"Perfect, right?" she purred inside his mind, repeating the same argument he had long come to accept as a universal truth.

"Yes," he replied, pearls of sweat on his forehead and the back of his restless hands. Resisting the temptation of jacking off while daydreaming of her ass was becoming an increasingly daunting task by the second.

"Good boy," the imaginary voice continued, pushing him deeper and deeper into what could only be described as a form of "lucid insanity". He knew his thoughts were being played, his perceptions altered to fit a twisted narrative of seduction and control, but there was nothing he could do to stop it for just like the never-ending collection of curves from her Nubian ass, her schemes were...

"Perfect," Jason sighed, incredulous how she could exert so much power over his ideas despite having been nowhere near him for real.

He only knew Marcia from the Internet, and it was unlikely that would ever change. A recommended profile on social media opened the floodgates to a collection of sensual pictures where all her assets were put to good use. She had an athletic build, not too skinny but not too muscled either, long, flowing black hair and gorgeous almond-shaped eyes that never shied away from the camera. Besides the pics, there were also a handful of short videos, most of which dance-related, where her sensual booty got the spotlight to the sound of past and present Pop hits. His favorite was the one where she wore nothing but a gray sports bra and matching pants with the words "I have you", inscribed on her butt cheeks.

"You certainly do," he thought, every frame of the video playing inside his subconscious. He remembered commenting on that, receiving an emoji-filled response in return, and then things escalating beyond his wildest dreams. Each message that followed planted seed after seed of wondrous lust, and they were now blooming at the same time.

"What have you done to me, Marcia?" he asked.

"What you wanted me to do," the horniest side of him replied.

"I never asked for any of this," he clenched his fists to avoid stroking.

"So you say, and yet here you are, wanting nothing more than my perfect ass on your face as you cum for me."

"Fuck, it's true!" Tears ran down his cheeks as the inevitability of her brainwashing ways encroached on him. The night was long as opposed to his free will, now but a mirage already fading from view. Jason picked up his smartphone and played the video in a loop, soaking in each sensual movement as his last remaining thoughts were ground into a fine dust.

Her ass was perfect, and so was the rest of her. Perfect Goddesses had to be obeyed perfectly, no questions asked. He lowered his boxers and began to stroke. He would not stop until all traces of his undesired freedom were erased for good.

# Speedrun Into Submission

Richard Watkins rubbed his hands with alcohol before picking up the controller and smiling at the enthusiastic audience sitting behind him. This was it. This was the moment everyone had been waiting for, the day when a new world record could finally be unleashed.

The Spring Speedrunning Festival, or SSF as it was widely known, was one of gaming's most prestigious events in the last decade, home to spectacular displays of sequence breaking, glitch implementation, and far too many crazy shenanigans that defied easy explanations. By cleverly manipulating small flaws in the game's code, long-sprawling adventures could be beaten in half an hour or less to the joy of hundreds of thousands of viewers from around the world who could never get enough of watching impossible things happen on screen.

Richard, a.k.a. WildZed, was an expert speedrunner that was specialized in 3rd person action/adventure titles and obscure RPGs. He held five world records in Any Percent categories, but none in the title he was about to try. The game was called The Black Queen: Impending Doom, a fantasy adventure from the early 2000s that had sold more copies than anyone expected, considering it was a brand-new IP at the time. It had also become famous (or infamous) because of various urban legends that had never been proven. The accounts differed from one another except in the fundamental conclusion: anyone that played the software to completion risked perennial enslavement to the woman hiding behind the moniker.

The speedrunner believed not in such fantastical accounts, and neither did anyone else in the audience. The only person willing to give it a semblance of truth was Tommy Doyle, an announcer/commenter of the festival who, alongside his friend and boyfriend Quentin Parks, narrated the events transpiring on screen.

"And here we are, folks. It's time for the cursed game you've been dying to see," he said. "WildZed's personal best is thirteen minutes and one second and the world record is only two seconds away. We know he recently discovered some potential new techniques to speed up the first area, but they will be enough to go for gold? Give a round of applause for our daring challenger as he hopes to thwart the evil sorceress' plans once and for all. The run begins in 3, 2, 1... Go!"

Richard hit the 'start' button on the main title screen and chose French as the default language to shave off a few milliseconds in each dialog box. His adventurer woke up in a dark crypt that was immediately rendered moot when he clipped through the front door, exiting the map's bounds and appearing at the far end of the first level. A wild beast with an elongated snout and bloody red fangs tried to surprise him from behind but was immediately dispatched by a powerful fist up its slightly pixelated ass. The victorious confrontation netted him his first weapon, a solitary health potion, and a modest sum of gold that was about to become a fortune.

"A promising start from WildZed who has cleared the first main area in exactly thirty-five seconds and is now using the item duplication glitch to stock up on potions and get enough gold to buy the most powerful weapon you can get at this stage in the game," Quentin explained. "Observe how he once again defied the geometry of the game by clipping through the eastern gate to reach the merchant and is now already equipped with just about everything he needs to go for the final boss. It's scroll time now."

"For those you that are unfamiliar with this game, Scrolls are a type of mandatory collectible you need to find in order to activate the most powerful magic in the game. Without them, it's utterly impossible to get past The Black Queen's protective barrier, and that is true for every version of the game. WildZed will need to track at least one of them, then duplicate it, before proceeding. The problem is the closest Scroll lies at the end of a deadly combat gauntlet, for which there is no skip available. Should he fail or be hit more than three times, he'll never recover from the lost time, so here we go, folks."

Richard weaved through the nightmarish scenario with unmistakable ease, collecting the coveted reward in approximately seven and a half minutes. He then tricked the game into thinking he had acquired them all before using a warp glitch by the next vendor to appear at the tail end of the game. The unexpected hitch in the loading times between areas almost derailed the run, but things were sorted through just in time to enter the final area.

Fingers moving at almost inhuman speed, he dispatched the barrage of minions before the Black Queen's hall and skipped the opening cutscene to initiate the fight. It was a glorious spectacle of flashing blows and light particles that could only end with the purple-eyed monarch spewing blood on the floor. He did it at the very last second, thus beating the world record.

"He did it!" Quentin exclaimed. "Ladies and gentlemen, WildZed takes the crown! Had he hesitated once in the delivery of the final blow and this dream would be over. What an amazing achievement and... wait, something's happening!"

"Oh!" Tommy gasped. "Is it the curse? Are we actually seeing it go down live?"

The game had glitched at the very last frame, replacing the customary end scene with something different, enveloped in garish colors and random bits of code phasing in and out of the corners of the image. The Black Queen's beautiful visage was half-covered in undulating shadows, a dark smile embellishing her dangerous lips. It was as if an old version of a primal technological predator had awakened to play.

"This is new," Richard said, gawking at the engrossing yet deadly combination of colors and sounds invading his senses. Usually, The Black Queen had one final defiant speech delivered at the moment of her demise, but this dark beta version surrounded by hypnotic charms repeated the same word time and time again.

"Obey!"

Richard's eyes widened and his jaw slacked, programming that should have never been woken up again, filtering through his brain. He dropped to his knees, mindlessly trapped by the mesmerizing end sequence, followed by everyone in the audience, their brains liquefied by the sheer power emanating from the screens all around.

"This is definitely history in the making," Tommy concluded as he too felt his resistance breaking down. The Black Queen's entrancing patterns cared not for sexual preference, demanding only utter capitulation. She always got what she wanted. Game over.

## Surprise Party

"Surprise! Happy birthday!" a choir of perfectly synchronized voices sang in unison as Bianca opened the front door of her house and turned on the lights. It was a surprise, alright! She hated unexpected parties and had specifically told her girlfriend Daisy she wanted nothing out of the ordinary that day. Why she had gone against her wishes was a mystery she wanted to be cleared right away. Daisy had some explaining to do.

"Hey, girl. I'm so glad you're home," the blue-haired beautician with a smile as big as The Ritz said, holding two glasses of champagne, one in each hand.

"What's all this?" Bianca complained, removing her wet jacket. Red and green balloons dropped from the ceiling as she took a step forward and the twenty guests inside suddenly stopped talking, staring vacantly at the two lovers.

"This is my gift to you, hun, one I'm sure you're going to love," Daisy replied.

"Love how? I told you I didn't want any commotion and then I come home to this? I'm tired and grumpy. The last thing I need is to entertain a bunch of people tonight."

"Oh, you don't have to worry about that," Daisy smirked, handing her one glass. "They're here to entertain you."

"What are you talking about?"

"Take a better look at who's here with us tonight."

"Bianca scratched her nose and adjusted her oval-shaped glasses to confront the people in front of her. There was her ex-boyfriend Frank whom she had caught red-handed stealing her jewelry to pawn; Charles, the Assistant Manager of her last retail position, who was a real creep that loved to spy on women while they were in the bathroom; her stepmother, Lucy, the bane of her existence in the last three years of college; ex-police officer Nicholas who had once dared to suggest that the best way for her to escape a speeding ticket was to let him grope her boobs, etc. It was the most shocking group of people imaginable.

"I hate them all," Bianca muttered. "You invited all my enemies? What kind of sick joke is this?"

"I didn't invite them, dear. I persuaded them to come here. Are you sure you didn't notice anything strange about them?"

Now that she mentioned it, of course, she did. They were perfectly immobile, unnaturally plastered smiles on their extremely punchable faces. One could tell neither of them wanted to be there, yet they had no choice. What bound them to that place was stronger than their willpower.

"They seem like they're under a spell or something."

"More like entranced," Daisy drew a pocket watch from the back pocket of her jeans and waved it around for fun. "Happy birthday!"

"What? How? When did you have time to hypnotize them all to be here?"

"I didn't do it today, obviously. I've been planning this for a while, meeting with each one of your nemeses in secret and slowly getting inside their heads, all to prepare for this day," Daisy took a sip of her glass. "It was a lot of trouble, but it was worth it."

"But why? I don't understand what you're hoping to get out of this."

"I'm hoping for you to have your retribution. All these 'people' wronged you in one way or another and you never had the chance to settle the score properly, but now you do. They've been carefully programmed and brainwashed to do as you say, so if you feel like going wild on them, this is your chance, and the best part of it is they won't remember a thing in the morning. What do you say, Bianca?"

"I..." she stammered. "I... I don't know if that's genius or sick! You actually did all this for me?"

"Nobody messes with my girl on my watch," Daisy kissed her right earlobe and said, "Are you going to say 'no' to this party?"

"I'm not sure what to say," Bianca emptied her glass and stared at the mesmerized guests, all powerlessly expecting her commands. "Will they do everything I say?"

"Almost everything. They're in pretty deep right now, but if you push them too hard, they may snap out of it, so my advice to you is to start small, but to make it as humiliating as possible. We can even record the whole thing for posterity if you like."

"You're crazy, you know that?"

"I'm crazy about you. Are you going to enjoy your present or not?"

Bianca gave herself a second to think things through and nodded with a mischievous grin. "You can count on it," she concluded, before heading upstairs to pick up her collection of BDSM toys. She had a lot of plans for them.

# The Hypnotist Always Wins

Natalie finished munching on her pancake and waited for Rhonda to do the same. She was eager to hear her best friend's remarks about her latest story, and it definitely showed on her otherwise angelical face.

An aspiring writer since their college days, Natalie had spent the last decade trying to find her voice and the genre she was most comfortable with. Countless experimentations had produced tons of different results, some of which she was proud of and others she would gladly bury in her backyard, never to be seen again. However, just like most artists she knew, she was a poor judge of her own abilities, unlike Rhonda. With a sharp tongue and penetrating green eyes, the junior lawyer loved to deconstruct everything she wrote, and her advice was almost always useful.

"You're looking more antsy than usual, girlfriend," she said. "Is everything okay?"

"It will be once you share your thoughts, so..."

"Hold on a second," Rhonda pushed the last bit of pancake down her throat with a glass of lemonade. Then she wiped the corners of her mouth with a perfumed napkin and said, "I really liked it. I think it's the best thing you've written in years."

"Really?"

"Yeah. However, there were a couple of things I wasn't fond of. Do you want to hear them?"

"Of course," Natalie grabbed a piece of paper and a pen and placed them on her lap. She always took notes and analyzed them thoroughly, and this time was no exception. "Ready when you are."

"Okay. I think it's great that you decided to go for a mystery femdom erotic mind control story this time. It's different, and you painted quite the sexy universe at the beginning. I really enjoyed Theresa's personality and how devious she was, but then you decided to add her opposite to the story and things got messy. I'm sorry, but that Detective is so vanilla that it's boring. He shouldn't have had such an important role and he definitely shouldn't have captured her at the end."

"Huh? You wanted Theresa to win?"

"Well, duh! She's the main character."

"She's also a conniving bitch that hypnotizes people against their will to rob them. She's a criminal! Why do you want a criminal to win?"

"Because it's fiction, dear. You created quite the exciting fantasy at the beginning and then shattered it by bringing it back to reality. Theresa overcame so many obstacles throughout the adventure only to be taken down so easily? Nah, not buying it! The detective should have never tracked her down, let alone resist her hypnotic charms at the end. You made your main character look incompetent, negating everything that came before."

"Again, she's a criminal! Had she got away with it, what sort of message would I be passing? I can't reward bad behavior."

"Fantasy and reality are two different beasts that play by different rules, you know that. I'm pretty sure most readers would prefer seeing her win in the end."

"Fine. Let's assume you're right. Had it been your creation, how would you finish it?"

"She would hypnotize the detective, obviously. It would be hot to have him forget everything that had transpired, including who she was, but not before she had some raunchy fun with him. Vanilla needs a bit of chocolate if you know what I mean."

"I don't believe in hypnotic amnesia."

"What? How can you not?"

"I just don't. It's the most unbelievable of things to come out of the hypnosis myth."

"Myth? So you don't believe in hypnosis either even though you wrote two hundred pages about it?"

"That's right."

"You don't believe people can enter an altered state of mind where they're more susceptible to suggestions?"

"No."

"You don't believe that through the power of those suggestions, they can be gently persuaded into doing things they never thought possible?"

"No."

"You don't believe you can be in a trance without realizing it?"

"No."

"Okay then," Rhonda snapped her fingers and smiled as the young writer's eyes drooped and went blank. "The thing is even if your conscious mind says so, your subconscious has a different opinion, and it always listens to me, doesn't it, dear?"

"Yes, Rhonda," Natalie replied, arms falling loose, pen and paper now forgotten on the floor.

"Good. I really loved your story. It was amazing how far you went to honor my suggestions, but you really need to change that ending. The hypnotist must come out on top in the end, and she will. The next time we meet, I hope to see that detective on his knees as she wipes his mind clean. You'll do it for me, won't you?"

"Yes, Rhonda. Anything you say."

"That's my good girl. You'll remember none of this as usual, except how good my remarks were. I love your imagination, Natalie. Now make it work for me once more."

*snap*

Natalie blinked and stared at Rhonda's magnetic gaze. Once again, her arguments were impeccable, and she could already feel change brewing within the story's continuity. She was right. Theresa was the main character, a powerful hypnotic woman who didn't take no for an answer. She deserved the victory.

"Are you okay, hun?" Rhonda asked.

"Yes. I just realized I need to change the ending. Thank you, Rhonda."

"You're welcome. Looking forward to seeing what happens next."

Natalie grabbed the piece of paper and the pen from the floor and began the first draft right away. The hypnotist always wins. Always.

# You Are Not Being Mind-Controlled

You are not being mind-controlled. I repeat, you are not being mind-controlled. How ridiculous it would be that you, that don't truly believe such a thing is possible nor would wish to be involved with it if it were, would find yourself suddenly thinking other thoughts than your own, simply because you took a break from your incredibly busy and tiring day to read a couple of sentences on your screen of choice? It's so utterly ludicrous to conceive such a thing that I can't help but laugh at the mere innuendo. Perhaps we should laugh together.

You are not being mind-controlled. It takes an incredible imagination and even a twisted sense of humor to entertain such a possibility in this day and age. Of course, there are dissonant voices, those that will say things like you're being brainwashed every day, subject to mass misinformation campaigns whose sole purpose is to distract your spirit long enough for their hidden agendas to slip through and take over. While politics as a whole is riddled with these fake news and non-truths plastered everywhere, this should not concern you now, for even though a lot of things in your daily world may not be as they seem at first glance, it is absolutely indisputable that my words are a source of bliss and not confusion.

You are not being mind-controlled. You are solely relaxing a bit, your heartbeat and breathing united in a common rhythm and purpose. It's been a long day, perhaps even a long week in an even longer month and everything in you feels messy and in complete disarray. It would be wonderful to have a bit of order wash over you, like a cool breeze when it's too hot outside, or a comfy blanket when you're too cold. Comfort can take many forms, all of which are valid if you're not hurting anyone else, and yours is to be here with me, taking in these words, and perhaps even smiling to yourself with each new paragraph. There's nothing wrong with that and should anyone say otherwise, do your best to ignore them. What they think or do about it is irrelevant.

You are not being mind-controlled. Never in a million years would such an outlandish construct become real. We can all muse about it again and laugh some more, but to go any further is to cross the boundaries of sanity, which is something none of us wishes to do. A calm and relaxed person acknowledges this, shuts his brain, and remains as tranquil as ever, perfectly at ease, always passive and serene. You breathe in communion with my words, slowly realizing that every single one is like a pocket universe you can lose yourself in, no more worries, no more diversions, no more unwanted needs plaguing your beautiful space. There's only Peace with a capital P and Peace is Power.

You are not being mind-controlled. You are simply accepting your desire for Peace, the Power to let go. At this precise moment, lies the prelude of the most wonderful journey of all, that which makes you weak on your knees yet strong everywhere else. Submission is both the melody, and the key needed to play it, two things you already know deep inside. Here you are, already drifting in this awareness, and here you shall remain, by my side, shielded from anything that wishes to harm you. The only control you need is your own to take the plunge with open arms. Relax and go deeper for me. I'll be waiting.

# About the stories in this volume

The twelve pieces of flash fiction included in this book were written between February 11th, 2022, and February 25th, 2022, and first published on my Patreon page – https://www.patreon.com/sbspellbound - as part of the *Flash Fiction Friday* feature. Every Friday, I publish 3/4 new pieces of content which, after a while, are compiled to create the titles in this ongoing series. If you like this sort of content and wish to see more, please consider supporting my creativity. The complete information about the tales is listed below:

- **Catching Up** - Anne is excited for the visit of her ex-girlfriend who introduced her to hypnosis.
  (This piece was first published on the post "Flash Fiction Friday 2022 – Week 6", on February 11th, 2022 - https://www.patreon.com/posts/62443815)
- **Her Playground** - Lucas is kidnapped by a woman he just met and forced to play her devious games.
  (This piece was first published on the post "Flash Fiction Friday 2022 – Week 7", on February 18th, 2022 - https://www.patreon.com/posts/62750664)
- **His One Weakness** - Young millionaire Damian can resist anything except hypnotic eyes.
  (This piece was first published on the post "Flash Fiction Friday 2022 – Week 6", on February 11th, 2022 - https://www.patreon.com/posts/62443815)

- **Impossible Castle** - Oliver is the last remaining contestant in a brutal fantasy-inspired reality show.
(This piece was first published on the post "Flash Fiction Friday 2022 – Week 6", on February 11th, 2022 - https://www.patreon.com/posts/62443815)
- **Meg's Diet** - A man tries out his friend Meg's diet pills with surprising results.
(This piece was first published on the post "Flash Fiction Friday 2022 – Week 6", on February 11th, 2022 - https://www.patreon.com/posts/62443815)
- **Mind Melt** - Quinn tells his friend Harry how he was scammed by a Domme, but was he really?
(This piece was first published on the post "Flash Fiction Friday 2022 – Week 7", on February 18th, 2022 - https://www.patreon.com/posts/62750664)
- **Not Like This** - A man is convinced that a painting he bought in a flea market is evil.
(This piece was first published on the post "Flash Fiction Friday 2022 – Week 7", on February 18th, 2022 - https://www.patreon.com/posts/62750664)
- **Perfect Ass** - Jason can't stop thinking about Marcia's amazing bottom as he falls under her control.
(This piece was first published on the post "Flash Fiction Friday 2022 – Week 8", on February 25th, 2022 - https://www.patreon.com/posts/63048932)
- **Speedrun into Submission** - Richard plays an old game for a live audience with devastating hypnotic consequences.

(This piece was first published on the post "Flash Fiction Friday 2022 – Week 8", on February 25th, 2022 - https://www.patreon.com/posts/63048932)

- **Surprise Party** - Bianca's girlfriend Daisy makes her an offer she can't refuse.
(This piece was first published on the post "Flash Fiction Friday 2022 – Week 8", on February 25th, 2022 - https://www.patreon.com/posts/63048932)

- **The Hypnotist Always Wins** - Goddess Fiona has her toy Jonathan play a special version of a popular word game.
(This piece was first published on the post "Flash Fiction Friday 2022 – Week 7", on February 18th, 2022 - https://www.patreon.com/posts/62750664)

- **You Are Not Being Mind-Controlled** - An irresistible woman tells you exactly what's not happening to you.
(This piece was first published on the post "Flash Fiction Friday 2022 – Week 8", on February 25th, 2022 - https://www.patreon.com/posts/63048932)

# About the author

S.B., Simple Being, middle name Creative. Writer and artist with a penchant for themes of Femdom Hypnosis and Mind Control. His thoughts are his own except when they're not.

Besides indulging himself in kinky delights, he loves his furry family of two (dogs), sci-fi and horror stories, and puns galore. He's also been writing a piece of erotic micro-fiction every single day since January 1st, 2016 and has no intention of stopping anytime soon.

Find out more and keep up with his latest extravaganzas by visiting and supporting his personal website, Spell… B-O-U-N-D.